Raghnall Bear
and the Game of
White Handkerchief

E.J. Wylie

AUSTIN MACAULEY PUBLISHERS™

LONDON ⋆ CAMBRIDGE ⋆ NEW YORK ⋆ SHARJAH

In the south of Scotland, you will find a park. Some call it magical, others call it ordinary, but Raghnall Bear calls it Home. The trees are thick in the centre of the forest, which is where he lives with all of his friends. Together, they play games, go on adventures and Raghnall Bear teaches them new and exciting things.

On one bright summer's day, in the middle of August, the leaves on the trees were thicker than usual. Raghnall Bear had been thinking of a new game to teach the others and decided that today would be the perfect day to try it out. He smiled, looking down at the notes of the game he had invented before eating some blackberries he had picked the day before. After he had finished them, he tucked the notepad and pencil containing the notes into his flannel, chequered shirt pocket and took his flat cap off a small branch stub. Putting the cap on his head, he walked down a narrow dirt track, whistling to himself.

He arrived at a group of bushes and paused, hearing some rummaging. He tilted his head and smiled as a stag emerged, eating some leaves.

'Morning, Stanley,' Raghnall Bear said, cheerfully.

'Mornin',' Stanley Stag replied, through a mouthful of leaves.

'I have a new game, where are the others?' asked Raghnall Bear, looking around.

'They're over there,' said Stanley Stag, pointing to his right with his antlers, having now finished his mouthful of leaves.

'Ah, so they are. Well, come on!' said Raghnall Bear, leading the way.

At the edge of the trees, there is a little clearing before the path. Gathered here, playing Tag were Timmy Terrier, Felix Fox, Helen Hedgehog and Neil Newt. Overlooking their game from a nearby oak tree was Oma Owl, who was "too old to join in such games". Instead, she looked down at them all lovingly, enjoying the sight of them having fun. Hearing footsteps, she looked up and saw Stanley Stag and Raghnall Bear make their way into the clearing. She smiled and flew down to join the others, who had stopped playing Tag upon their arrival.

'Gather 'round now. I have a new game for you,' said Raghnall Bear in his soft, Scottish accent. He is rather rugged, as bears go, but we'll put that down to all the adventures he has had.

'What's the game?' Helen Hedgehog asked excitedly. She loved games and considered herself the best at them. They all gathered around to hear the rules of this new game.

'It's called "White Handkerchief",' Raghnall Bear said, pulling a white handkerchief out of his grey trouser pocket and gently waving it.

'Oh, I love this game!' Helen Hedgehog declared, jumping up and down.

'You can't do. We haven't played it before,' Felix Fox said, matter-of-factly.

Helen Hedgehog stopped jumping up and down and looked sad before eagerly asking, 'How do we play?'

'Well, one player has to count to 50…' Raghnall Bear began.

'I'll do it!' Timmy Terrier yapped, walking to stand next to Raghnall Bear, his tail wagging.

'Right oh!' chuckled Raghnall Bear. 'Well, you count to 50 and the rest of us will go and hide. Once you have reached 50, yell "LOOKING", so we know to stop moving and come and find us.'

'Easy,' Timmy Terrier exclaimed, boastfully.

'Yes, but the game gets harder,' Raghnall Bear said, smiling at the others, pleased he had created a game to challenge and entertain them. 'If you find one of us, we have to go and sit on that bench as we have been "Seen!",' Raghnall Bear pointed to the nearby bench.

'But!' he exclaimed quickly before he was interrupted by the others, keen to start the game. 'We can be "Freed" by the other hiders waving a white handkerchief… or a paw, foot or hoof… at the "Caught" player. If the "Caught" player sees the wave, they shout "WHITE HANDKERCHIEF" as loud as they can. The "Searcher" has to stop looking, close their eyes and count to 20. Once you have shouted "White Handkerchief", you can run and hide again. However, if you wave to someone and are "Seen!" while doing so, even if the other player is in the middle of shouting "White Handkerchief", you are also "Caught" and must sit on the bench. If more than one of you is on the bench, only one of you has to shout, "White Handkerchief" to all be "Freed".'

'Oh, this sounds fun!' exclaimed Helen Hedgehog. 'Will you play with us?' she asked Oma Owl.

'Yes, I think I will,' Oma Owl replied, gently but with a hint of competitiveness.

'Yay!' squealed Helen Hedgehog.

'One…' started Timmy Terrier, forcibly. He liked to get games started straight away as that meant more playing time, which he loved. 'Two…'

'Everyone hide!' Raghnall Bear called, over the counting.

Stanley Stag galloped into the thickest part of the trees and laid on the ground. He put his head down to hopefully disguise his antlers as tree roots. There are disadvantages to being tall and Stanley Stag discovered that hiding was one of them. Neil Newt, on the other hand, loved hiding games as he was so small he could hide almost anywhere without being seen. He decided that it would be unfair to hide under a rock in the pond and so settled for trying to disguise himself on a nearby lamppost, high up, not wanting to be accidentally stood on.

Helen Hedgehog scurried to her favourite hiding place, in the middle of a big bush and curled up into a prickly ball. Felix Fox slinked off to a hedge near the bench so he could watch what happened in the game. Raghnall Bear also hid near the bench so that he could wave to "Caught" players. The tree Oma Owl lives in is very thick, so he hid behind that. Oma Owl, herself, decided to hide behind a rock on the ground, thinking that Timmy Terrier would look for her in the sky, not the ground. And thus began the game of "White Handkerchief".

'…50! READY OR NOT, HERE I COME!' yelled Timmy Terrier with glee. He scampered off up the path towards a large group of bushes. There, he went on all fours and crawled into the bush. Helen Hedgehog, curled up in her ball, heard Timmy Terrier approach. She remained still and silent but could feel him get closer.

'Seen,' whispered Timmy Terrier suddenly, smirking.

'Not fair!' pouted Helen Hedgehog, unfurling quickly.

'Shouldn't hide so obvious then!' laughed Timmy Terrier.

'I didn't,' retorted Helen Hedgehog, annoyed that she got "Caught" so quickly.

'You always hide here,' chuckled Timmy Terrier, backing out of the bush with Helen Hedgehog following him.

Once into the open, Timmy Terrier scurried off in search of someone else and Helen Hedgehog grudgingly went over and sat next to the bench. She looked at the floor, sulking, before remembering that she could be "Freed". Suddenly a lot happier, she looked around expectantly but didn't see anyone apart from Timmy Terrier, snooping around the rest of the bushes.

Seeing Helen Hedgehog next to the bench, Raghnall Bear got his white handkerchief out of his pocket and, smiling to himself, waved it around the side of the tree. Unfortunately for Helen Hedgehog and Raghnall Bear, Helen Hedgehog had been so busy watching Timmy Terrier that she didn't see the wave. However, Timmy Terrier, discovering there was no one else in the bushes, turned to look in the trees and did see the wave.

'SEEN!' he called across the park with glee.

Surprised, Raghnall Bear turned around to see Timmy Terrier bounding over.

He laughed when he saw how happy Timmy Terrier was.

'I saw you wave!' Timmy Terrier gushed.

'So you did, go and find the others then,' chuckled Raghnall Bear.

He made his way over to the bench and sat down on it next to Helen Hedgehog.

'Oh, we'll never be "Freed",' she despaired.

'We'll have to keep a look out. I'll take this side, you take that one,' suggested Raghnall Bear.

'Good idea,' said Helen Hedgehog, scanning her side of the landscape for any sign of movement.

Meanwhile, Timmy Terrier had made it to the pond and was trying to look over the edge without falling in. He thought Neil Newt might be hiding there as it is somewhere he likes to go but Timmy Terrier couldn't see him. All of a sudden, he heard…

'WHITE HANDKERCHIEF!' shouted from Helen Hedgehog. Felix Fox, who had been watching the whole game, decided that he should free the others and snuck out of his hiding place to wave at them.

The shout surprised Timmy Terrier so much that he lost his balance and fell in the pond! Swimming to the bank, he managed to get out and shake the water off himself. He sat down and counted to 10, deciding that falling in the pond meant he could take some time off his counting.

Raghnall Bear and Helen Hedgehog rushed to hide again. She decided to hide in a different bush this time, convinced that she wouldn't be "Caught" again while Raghnall Bear went back to the tree. He didn't mind if he was "Caught", he was just happy they were all enjoying his game.

'…20! READY OR NOT, HERE I COME!' shouted Timmy Terrier, keen for the game to finish now he was cold and wet.

He ran back to the first bush he went to but couldn't see Helen Hedgehog there. Smiling to himself at the challenge of finding her, he turned around and headed towards the trees, thinking she might have gone in there. He weaved around them, looking right and left as he went before tripping over some tree roots and landing on them.

'Ouch!' the tree roots said, making Timmy Terrier jump off them and back away. Only, they were not tree roots at all, but Stanley Stag who sat up, rubbing his head where his antlers were.

'Sorry,' laughed Timmy Terrier, relieved that it was only Stanley Stag and not some kind of tree monster.

'S'pose I'm "Seen" then?' Stanley Stag said, disappointed that his hiding place had not worked out.

'Yes, seen!' called Timmy Terrier, gleefully.

They went back to the bench together as Timmy Terrier was sure someone would try to free Stanley Stag and that he would catch them when they did. Stanley Stag sat next to the bench, looking around while Timmy Terrier stood, ready to run, doing the same. The sun had dried him off and he had "Caught" someone, so he was enjoying the game again. After some time, no one had come to wave, so Timmy Terrier decided to pretend he was looking for them but actually kept an eye out for someone coming to "Free" Stanley Stag.

He went towards the bushes closest to the bench and had a little look. His eyes kept darting towards the bench, making sure he didn't miss anything. On the third time of doing this, he saw Raghnall Bear's head emerge around the corner of the big oak tree.

'SEEN!' yell Timmy Terrier, looking directly at him. Raghnall Bear jumped, smiled and walked towards the bench and sat down. He, however, was not the only person who jumped at Timmy Terrier's yell. Poor Helen Hedgehog was curled up hidden under a leaf in the bush that Timmy Terrier was pretending to look in. At his sudden yell, she jumped and squealed in fright, revealing her hiding place.

'Ah! Seen,' laughed Timmy Terrier, shocked at finding Helen Hedgehog right under his nose. She went over to the bench, still shaking. Raghnall Bear put her in his lap to make her feel safe and they all looked out together.

Timmy Terrier, having now "Caught" half of the players, was sure someone would reveal themselves to rescue them so started pacing up and down in front of the bench. Now, Felix Fox could see everything going on as he had hidden in the hedge near the bench, and Neil Newt was on a nearby lamppost so had some idea, but Oma Owl was unsure. She had heard two people be "Caught" and nothing else seemed to be happening so decided to investigate. Slowly, she backed away from the rock and the nearby trees and took off, flying low to try and stay hidden. Neil Newt had also realised that no one was going to help rescue them, so decided to start climbing down from the lamppost.

Oma Owl flew around the back of the trees to stay hidden and landed on the hedge near the lamppost. Unfortunately, for her, Timmy Terrier heard the noise and spun around.

'Seen!' he called.

'Oh,' signed Oma Owl, who then flew to the bench and sat down next to Raghnall Bear.

'There's only Felix Fox and Neil Newt to rescue us now!' Helen Hedgehog moaned.

'I'm sure they will,' comforted Oma Owl.

They sat there, each looking out for one of the others. The forest was quiet except for the occasional high pitched "Beep Boop" from Raghnall Bear. It made Helen Hedgehog smile whenever he did and jealous that she could never do it the same.

Suddenly, there was a DING noise from the lamppost. Neil Newt had climbed down to the bottom, got a stone and climbed back up to the widest part. He had thrown the stone against the lamppost to create a noise to attract their attention and waved energetically. Everyone on the bench and Timmy Terrier, who was still guarding it, looked straight at the lamppost.

'WHI…' began Stanley Stag, Oma Owl and Helen Hedgehog.

'SEEEEN!' called Timmy Terrier, as loud as he could over the others.

'Ohhh,' Helen Hedgehog said as they stopped mid-shout.

Neil Newt joined the others on the bench. Felix Fox, still hidden in the hedges, wondered how best to "Free" the others. He snuck out from the back of the hedge and threw a stick into the trees to create a diversion. He then ran around the hedge and straight into Timmy Terrier, who hadn't moved but was looking directly at the spot the noise had come from.

'Ah!' Felix Fox shouted and tried to run back, surprised that he hadn't followed the noise.

'Seen!' called Timmy Terrier, equally surprised to see Felix Fox.

'I win!' exclaimed Timmy Terrier, turning to look at Raghnall Bear for confirmation.

'So you do! Well done.' Raghnall Bear said, smiling. And that concluded the first game of "White Handkerchief", which went on to become one of their favourite games to play together.

The Rules

- One person counts to 50

- Everyone else hides

- The 'Searcher' looks for people

- The 'Hiders' aren't allowed to move from their hiding place

- If found, 'Hiders' have to sit on the bench - they are 'Caught'

- Other 'Hiders' can wave a white handkerchief (or hand, foot, etc) to 'Free' the 'Caught' players

- If the wave is spotted, the 'Caught' player(s) yells 'White Handkerchief"

- The 'Searcher' then stops, covers their eyes and counts to 20

- All 'Hiders' on the bench can go and hide again

- The game continues until everyone is caught by the 'Searcher'

THE END

For Grandpa, thank you for the great memories.

About the Author

E.J. Wylie graduated from University of Derby in July 2017. Throughout her time there, she wrote her first book *Raghnall Bear and the Game of White Handkerchief*, while getting her degree in Film Production. She spends her free time writing, working on film shoots and drinking tea.

Acknowledgements

I would firstly like to thank everyone at Austin Macauley Publishers for making this publication possible. I would especially like to thank Stefanie Seaton for being so nice and helpful and answering all my questions and emails and taking an interest in my book. I would also like to thank the rest of the editorial team (Rebecca Ponting and Kirsty-Ellen Smillie) for also believing in my book. I would also like to thank the great illustrators for bringing my characters to life.

Secondly, I would like to thank my grandma and my dad for their support, encouragement and for helping to make the publication of this book possible. It means a lot to me, so thank you; I love you. I hope you enjoy the book; this is for you both.

And lastly, I would like to thank Kirsty Patrick for putting up with me stressing about which photo to use, how to word my blurb, etc. If there was a character that was a rock, it would be you.

First Published (2019)
Austin Macauley Publishers Ltd
25 Canada Square
Canary Wharf
London
E14 5LQ

ISBN 9781788789394 (Paperback)
ISBN 9781528956451 (ePub e-Book)

www.austinmacauley.com